Dear Parent:

Congratulations! Your child is taking the first steps on an exciting journey. The destination? Independent reading!

STEP INTO READING® will help your child get there. The program offers books at five levels that accompany children from their first attempts at reading to reading success. Each step includes fun stories, fiction and nonfiction, and colorful art. There are also Step into Reading Sticker Books, Step into Reading Math Readers, Step into Reading Write-In Readers, Step into Reading Phonics Readers, and Step into Reading Phonics First Steps! Boxed Sets—a complete literacy program with something to interest every child.

Learning to Read, Step by Step!

Ready to Read Preschool–Kindergarten
• big type and easy words • rhyme and rhythm • picture clues
For children who know the alphabet and are eager to begin reading.

Reading with Help Preschool–Grade 1
• basic vocabulary • short sentences • simple stories
For children who recognize familiar words and sound out new words with help.

Reading on Your Own Grades 1–3
• engaging characters • easy-to-follow plots • popular topics
For children who are ready to read on their own.

Reading Paragraphs Grades 2–3
• challenging vocabulary • short paragraphs • exciting stories
For newly independent readers who read simple sentences with confidence.

Ready for Chapters Grades 2–4
• chapters • longer paragraphs • full-color art
For children who want to take the plunge into chapter books but still like colorful pictures.

STEP INTO READING® is designed to give every child a successful reading experience. The grade levels are only guides. Children can progress through the steps at their own speed, developing confidence in their reading, no matter what their grade.

Remember, a lifetime love of reading starts with a single step!

Princess Story Collection

www.randomhouse.com/kids/disney

www.stepintoreading.com

Educators and librarians, for a variety of teaching tools, visit us at www.randomhouse.com/teachers

ISBN: 978-0-7364-2486-8

MANUFACTURED IN CHINA   10 9 8 7 6 5 4 3 2 1   First Edition

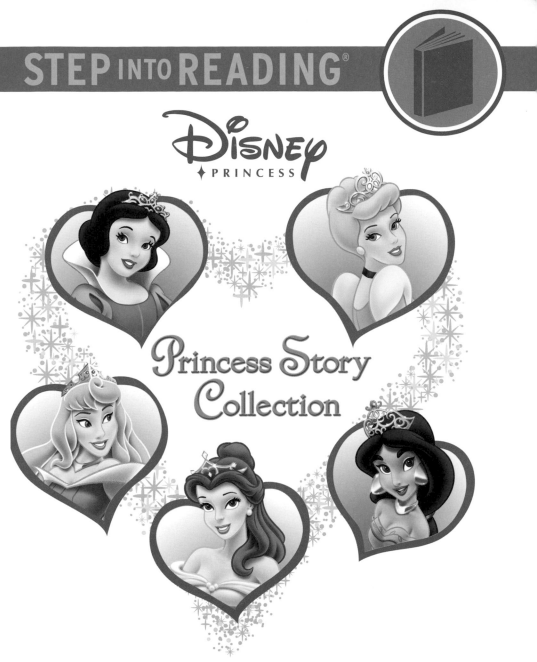

Disney
PRINCESS

Princess Story Collection

Step 1 and Step 2 Books

A Collection of Five Early Readers

Random House 🏠 New York

Contents

Cinderella's Countdown
to the Ball. 9

Friends for a Princess. 39

A Pony for a Princess.....69

Surprise for a Princess....99

A Pet for a Princess 129

STEP INTO READING®

STEP 1

WALT DISNEY'S

Cinderella

Cinderella's
Countdown TO THE Ball

By Heidi Kilgras

Illustrated by Atelier Philippe Harchy

Poor Cinderella.

Poof!

A fairy godmother.

One magic coach.

Two coachmen.

Three wishes
come true!

Four horses.

Five miles
to the ball.

Six royal doormen.

Seven men
want to dance.

Eight ladies
wait in line.

The Prince!

They meet.

They dance.
Nine ladies whisper.

Ten fingers touch.

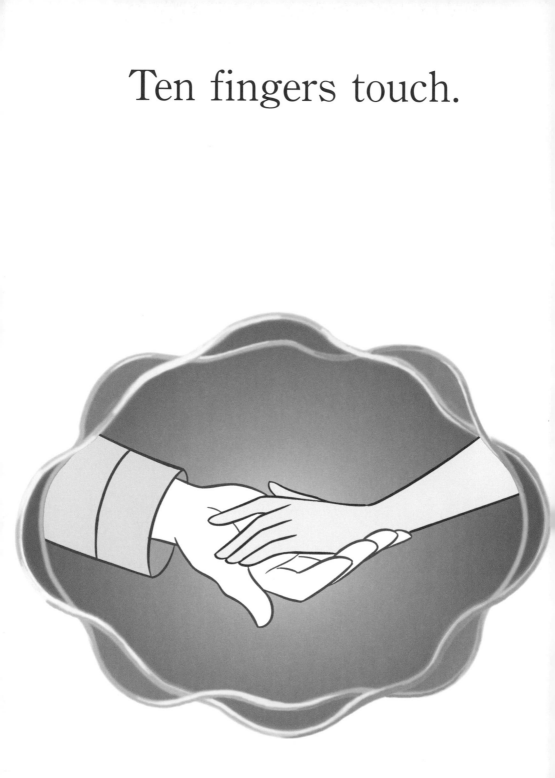

Eleven stars twinkle.

The clock chimes twelve times!

BONG
BONG
BONG
NG

Run, Cinderella!

One glass slipper.

Tap, tap.

Too small!

Crash!

The other slipper!

It fits!

Happily ever after!

The End

Friends for a Princess

By Melissa Lagonegro

Illustrated by Atelier Philippe Harchy

Snow White has
seven little friends.
Loving, kind,
and special friends.

Some have big beards.

Some have small.

Dopey has no
beard at all.

Doc is caring.

Doc is wise.

Doc needs glasses
for his eyes.

Happy is
the cheerful guy.

Bashful is

so very shy.

Sneezy always
has to sneeze.

Grumpy is
so hard to please.

Sleepy likes to
take a nap.

Dopey wears a
purple cap.

All the Dwarfs
work in a mine.

Then they march
home in a line.

Snow White is there
when they come back.

She welcomes them
and makes a snack.

The jolly friends
dance through the night.

The Seven Dwarfs
love sweet Snow White.

PRINCESS

A Pony
for a
Princess

By Andrea Posner-Sanchez

Illustrated by Francesc Mateu

Belle picked out a book
from the castle library.

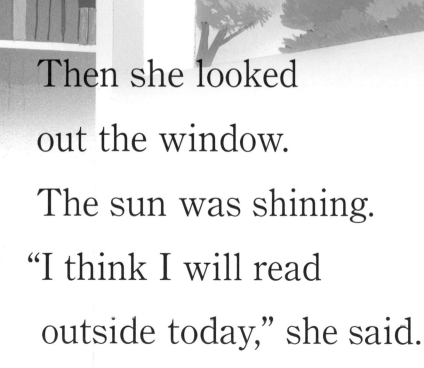

Then she looked
out the window.
The sun was shining.
"I think I will read
outside today," she said.

Belle left the castle.

She walked past the barn.

There was a big

pile of hay

by the barn.

She walked past
the apple tree.
There was a big
basket of apples
under the tree.

Belle sat down to read.

Belle read and read.
Before long,
she felt hungry.

Belle put down her book.

She walked back

to the castle

to get some lunch.

Belle put a sandwich,
some lemonade,
and some sugar cubes
into a picnic basket.

"And I will pick
   an apple for dessert,"
she said.

Belle went back outside.

She walked past the barn.

The hay was gone!

"That is odd," Belle said.

She walked past
the apple tree.
The basket was empty!

"Who could have
eaten all the apples?"
Belle asked.

Belle looked this way.

Belle looked that way.

Then she saw something

behind a bush.

It was a wild pony!

Belle stepped closer.

But the pony was scared.

It ran this way . . .

. . . and it ran that way.

But the pony would not

come to Belle.

Belle had an idea.
She took the sugar cubes
from the picnic basket.
She placed them in a row
on the grass.

Then she stepped back.

The pony ate one
sugar cube.

Then it ate another.
And another.

Soon the pony was
right next to Belle!

Belle held out the last sugar cube. The pony ate it right from her hand!

She reached out to pat

the pony's soft nose.

Belle was happy.
She led the pretty pony
to the barn.

And before long,
the princess and
the pony became
great friends.

DISNEP
♦PRINCESS

Surprise
for a
Princess

By Jennifer Liberts Weinberg
Illustrated by Peter Emslie
and Elisa Marrucchi

Once upon a time
there was a girl
named Briar Rose.

She lived in
the forest with
three fairies.
Their names were
Flora, Fauna,
and Merryweather.

One day,
the fairies sent
Briar Rose out
to pick berries.

While she was gone,
they planned
a surprise.

"Let's have a party
for Briar Rose,"
said Merryweather.
"With a cake!"
said Fauna.

"And a dress
fit for a princess,"
said Flora.

Flora began
to make the dress.

She cut.

She pinned.

She trimmed.

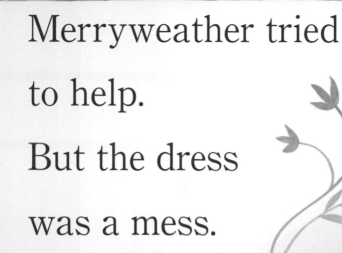

Merryweather tried
to help.
But the dress
was a mess.

There was too
much cloth.
And there were too
many bows.

"Oh, no!"
said Fauna.
"It is awful!"
said Merryweather.

Fauna began
to make the cake.
She read from
a cookbook.
It said she needed
eggs, flour,
and milk.

Fauna mixed.

And spilled.

And dribbled.

And dropped.

The milk dripped
onto the floor.
And the eggs
rolled off the table!
<u>Crack!</u>

At last the cake
was baked and iced.
But the icing slid
off the top.
And the candles
would not stand up.

"It is awful!"
said Merryweather.
"A flop!"
said Flora.

The fairies began
to worry.
Briar Rose was
coming home soon.

"I know just
the trick,"
said Merryweather.

She gave each fairy
a wand.
"Magic!"
they cried.
With a wave
of their wands . . .

<u>Poof!</u>

The cottage was clean as a whistle.

<u>Poof!</u>

The cake
was as pretty
as a picture.

Poof!

The dress

was fit

for a princess.

Briar Rose came home.
"Happy birthday!"
cried the fairies.

"Thank you!"
said Briar Rose.
"This is the
best surprise ever!"

The End

DISNEY
✦ PRINCESS

A Pet for a Princess

By Melissa Lagonegro

Illustrated by Atelier Philippe Harchy

Jasmine was
sad and lonely.
She needed a friend.

"Poor Jasmine,"
said her father.
"I want to make
you happy."

The next day,
he gave Jasmine
a big gift.
"Open it," he said.

Jasmine pulled off
the red sheet.

It was a tiger cub!

"I will call you Rajah,"
said Jasmine.
She was very happy.

Jasmine and Rajah
did many things
together.

They sat in the sun.

They watched
butterflies.

They played
lots of games.

Jasmine took good care
of Rajah.

She fed him.

She brushed him.

She gave him
lots of love.

Jasmine liked
to rub and scratch
his furry belly.
Rajah liked it, too!
Purrrrr!

The princess kept Rajah
safe from harm.

And she loved to play dress-up with him.

Jasmine made Rajah
a cozy little bed.
At night,
they fell fast asleep.

As time passed,
Rajah grew bigger . . .

and bigger . . .

. . . and bigger!

Rajah became
a <u>very</u> big tiger.
And a strong
tiger, too!

Now Rajah keeps
Jasmine safe
from harm.

Rajah is too big
to play dress-up.

He is too big

for his cozy little bed.

But he will never be
too big for a belly rub . . .

. . . or a hug!